Nothing to Fear from the Dark, my Dear

Written by
Traci Dunham

Illustrated by
Hannah Tuohy

Something Beautiful Inside

TAD BOOKS

TAD Books
www.tadbooks.com

Published by TAD Books
Haddonfield, NJ 08033

ISBN 978-0-9969538-1-8

Library of Congress Control Number:
2016907067

Printed in China

Mom, for reassuring me all those nights when I was afraid of the dark, and letting me know there was nothing to fear.

Jennifer Cannon and Alicia DiFabio, for editing my work. The changes you made were implemented and helped to improve the structure and flow of the story.

Moonwriters, for your friendship, support and insight.

John Young, for your input and editing skills.

Are you afraid at night, when there's no light? I hear the howling of the wind. I pull the covers up to my chin.

I hear tapping on the window panes; it's the branches
from the trees and the pattering of the rain.

Then lightning comes to brighten
my room. Clapping of thunder,

BOOM!

BOOM,

BOOM,

I jump out of bed and run down the
hall. Mama wakes up and tells me,
"There's nothing to fear from the dark, my dear."

Back in my room, I start to fall asleep.
Suddenly I hear footsteps,

CREAK,

CREAK.

CREAK,

I get up and look around to see what is making that
squeaking sound. I crack open my door and look out,
"Who's there?" I ask with a shout.

By the light of the moon, I see it's my sister walking to her room.

As I climb back in bed, I notice the open closet door.

There could be a monster in there, for sure.

Mama comes in and opens that door. All I see
are my toys on the floor. "See," Mama says,
"There's nothing to fear from the dark, my dear."

But, when Mama leaves, I start to dread, "What if there is something under my bed?" I could jump down and take a peek, "But what if something grabs my feet?"

As I bend down and take a look, I see
nothing but my favorite book.

As I lay back down I hear a **bump, bump, bump** and a **thump, thump, thump.**

"Oh no," I start to fear, "What are those other sounds I hear?" I yell for Mama who comes rushing in, "Why are you awake again?"

"I hear a **bump, bump, bump** and a **thump, thump, thump.**"

"Listen," Mama says and hugs me tight,
"It's just the clanging of the heater that
woke you up and caused a fright."

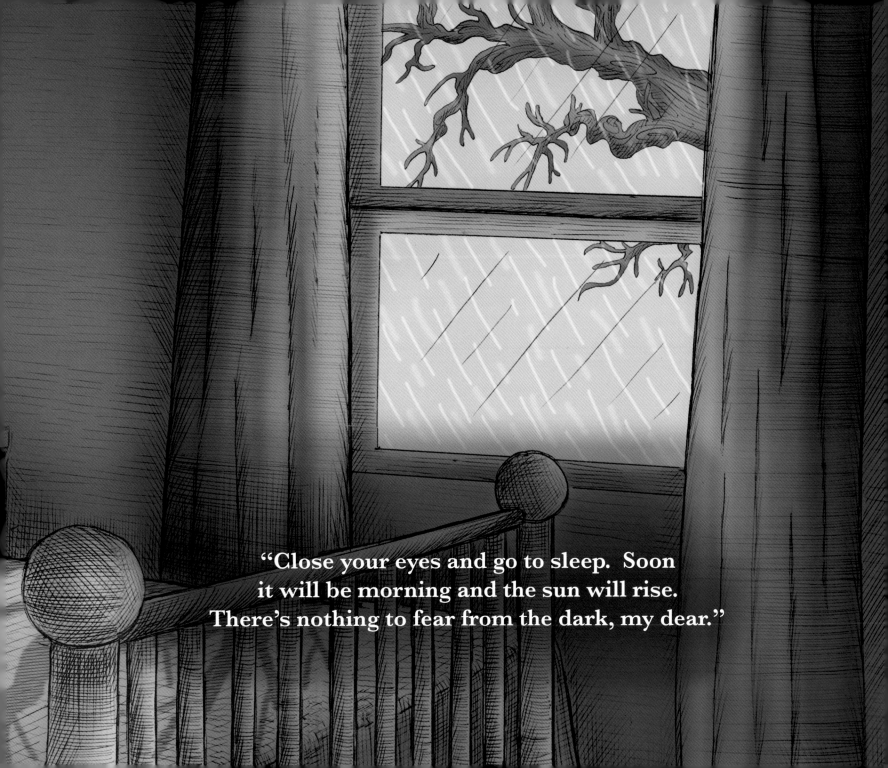

"Close your eyes and go to sleep. Soon
it will be morning and the sun will rise.
There's nothing to fear from the dark, my dear."

The sun streams through my window. I open my eyes. I look around. There is nothing to hear, no, not a sound.

Morning has come and I get out of bed.
Tonight, I'll remember what Mama said.

About the Author

Traci Dunham is a #1 best selling author, who resides in Haddonfield, NJ with her husband Sandy and her two daughters, Caroline and Paige. She spends her summers at the Jersey Shore in Wildwood Crest. This is Traci's third book and in 2015 she started her own publishing company TAD Books. Traci is a graduate of The College of New Jersey and a member of SCWBI.

Other Books by Traci Dunham

My Sister Lulu and Me

My Sister Lulu and Me is a heartwarming story that lets every child know that they are uniquely special. The story offers a vehicle for parents and teachers to open up a dialogue with children about accepting others with disabilities.

The Oyster's Secret

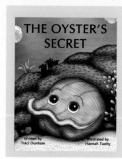

The Oyster's Secret is a beautifully illustrated book that teaches youngsters the importance of inner beauty. Through Mr. Oyster, young readers will learn that what is on the outside is not what counts; true beauty lies within.

About the Illustrator

Hannah Tuohy is an illustrator of over 21 children's books. She is a graduate of Oklahoma State University and a member of SCBWI. Her books include *No Sand in the House, Consider the Consequences* and *Ted and Pad Trick or Treat.* Hannah lives and works in Tulsa, Oklahoma with her husband, Justin. This is her third children's book collaboration with Traci.

TAD Books

Something Beautiful Inside

TAD BOOKS

TAD Books was established in 2015 by Traci Dunham. This publishing company was set up to help show children the great characteristics inside them through the books they read. Traci is available for public speaking engagements, school visits, book reading and signing events. For more information visit www.tadbooks.com and Facebook page TAD books. You can also email Traci at Traci@tadbooks.com.